# WHEN WINTER WEIGHS HEAVY

*When Winter Weighs Heavy*

Published by The Conrad Press Ltd. in the United Kingdom 2021

Tel: +44(0)1227 472 874
www.theconradpress.com
info@theconradpress.com

ISBN 978-1-914913-15-0

Copyright © Madeleine Reed, 2021

Cover illustration and map © Sue Reed

The moral right of Madeleine Reed to be identified as author of this work has been asserted in accordance with the Copyright, Designs and Patents Act 1988.

All rights reserved.

Printed and bound in Great Britain by Clays Ltd, Elcograf S.p.A

Typesetting and Cover Design by The Book Typesetters
www.thebooktypesetters.com

The Conrad Press logo was designed by Maria Priestley.

# WHEN WINTER WEIGHS HEAVY

## Madeleine Reed

Dedicated to my father, who motivated and advised me,
And to my twin, Bear, who is undoubtedly my muse.

# Chapter One

## Starving

I remember one evening a few winters ago, at Solstice, when a bitter wind blew through the walls and ice crept up woollen stockings and windowpanes. Everyone in the village shivered in the tiny local temple to sing thanks for the green things and for the promise of new life. We sang 'while the Great Bear hibernates', 'waiting for the cubs of spring' and 'the She-Bear will not sleep forever'. When the Silence fell on us all, I could hear the howling elements outside and the chattering of many teeth. The chattering of *so* many teeth that it barely felt like the Silence at all. Under my cloak, I wrung my hands, just to check that they were still there – they were so numb. And the teeth, echoing round the little temple like we were all still singing under our breath.

That's the sound I hear now. A rattling, clacking, echoing noise, muffled through the window. Outside, in the cool light of an autumn morning, the tithe carts lump past behind the clicking hooves of the king's donkeys. This year, as every year, he'll take away all our best. This year, as every year, the She-Bear will turn away, will go to sleep, will begin to settle down for winter, and She won't see us starving as we pray in the temple for mercy. As we pray that perhaps next year, he won't take so much. That next year, we'll have a new king.

That's treason, I realise, my fingers spread over my chest.

Did I just pray for death? Tonight, I'll hunt a sacrifice for the Great She-Bear. The donkeys all wear the king's crest. On a banner streaming out behind the tithe gatherers, the City Script reads *LONG LIVE THE KING*.

'Come away from the window,' my mother calls, so I settle back down to my needle and thread. Next year, surely, next year, there will be enough food.

On Saturday, the High Day, I give a rabbit to the She-Bear. The priest in the temple reads us the harvest thanksgivings from the Ursulaic Laws and when it's over, we sing 'joy, joy in times of plenty' and 'bless the king as he serves the Bear'. Bless the king indeed. Bless him and his clawing hands, the shadow of his greedy arms reached out to snatch and steal. Bless his snarling words of kindness to the subjects he abuses. Bless his rotten heart, so the Bear might take him into hibernation with Her. Bless the king.

The distant peaks glimmer in the evening sun. When I was a child, all muddy-faced and arrogant, I desperately wanted to travel to the Invius Mountains, jagged and blue, jutting out of the horizon, the king's winter retreat and a natural border between us, the Bear's people, and the western barbarians of the forests. It's said that they worship wolves and hunt bears for fun. So weak a god to hunt our powerful Mother! It's no surprise they're half crazy. And yet, I wonder if they say the same of us. After all, we tame their precious wolves and keep them as pets, as possessions. How humiliating.

The Invius Mountains seem to quiver as the sun sets behind them and they reach out over the country, casting dusky shadows on our towns, farms, fields and cities. Miles away, the king himself will also soon be hidden beneath the claws of the towering peaks. I remember my mother telling me stories of the last king. He was fine, she said. Just fine. Nothing special. Nothing changed under him; everything settled into a routine, a norm, a status quo of *'just fine'*. His son, who is now king, was a catch among the young ladies. He is only a few years older than Mother and, twenty or so years ago, many of her friends desperately desired to be his wife.

'I bless the Bear I'm not, now,' she would laugh.

Becoming king changed the young prince. Now, how many yearn for that era of 'fine' to return!

'Don't speak a word against the king,' warns the priest every High Day. 'He has the ears of the Great Bear Herself and an arm just as strong. He is Her Anointed and he is our sovereign. Remember, it is written, *the Great Bear giveth us a Leader and unto this Leader we giveth ourselves. Giveth thyself to the Bear's Anointed and by doing, thou givest thyself to the Bear.*' Mother says it was the old kings who wrote the Ursulaic Laws, so of course it would say that. I don't know what to think; I just want to enjoy my own harvest. I don't want to starve.

The sun gives a final brilliant flash, glancing off the wide, lazy river that snakes up the eastern hills, and then vanishes, dipping into obscurity with the glory and decadence of the Great Bear curling up in Her hibernation. I close the window shutters; it's going to be a cold night. Outside, an awful owl hoots and the distant sounds of laughter and conversations drifting up from the tavern confirm the corruption of the tithe gatherers.

'Sleep as She does,' Mother wishes me as I head upstairs. She sits at her spinning wheel with a single dancing candle.

But when I lay down in bed, I listen still to the revellers and I wonder if I can do anything as She does. I imagine the Bear crashing into the tavern, upsetting tables and splitting the cider barrels. I almost hear the screams and, as I lie awake staring at the ceiling, I see in the shadows the blank laughing faces of those royal thieves staring right back, and long red stripes tear open their beautiful linen tunics and their soft, pale skin. It is written, *the Great Bear eateth when She hungereth after food. The Great Bear drinketh when She thirsteth after water. The Great Bear killeth when She lusteth after life. Be likewise as the Great Bear and act only in thy need.*

We work all summer to store food for the winter, so that we can survive during the darkest, coldest months, full of illness and death. During winter, as the Bear sleeps, we rest from our labour, concentrating on simply surviving. That's what the Ursulaic Laws command, anyway. The king, from his comfortable winter retreat in the Invius Mountains, demands such a high tithe that we all work right through the winter now. I've never known a peaceful winter like the one the Laws describe.

Come morning, bands of hunters, foragers and traders come and go through the square. I join a group of other women, trailing behind the tithe carts, gathering what the wind returns to us. Some of the women have earned a pretty penny or two by sitting on knees and blushing at the tavern last night. Some tried and failed. Some of the older women sold pickles and preserves and others stole them back again. We follow them all morning, then we take the afternoon to return home. This is now an annual tradition, as natural as summer and winter Solstice, as engrained as weddings and funerals. Once home, we go back to our everyday business. It's as though the tithe carts never came, except our storehouses are emptier. It's sickening how normal this is. Does nobody care? Is this how life is meant to be?

When the sun goes down, I'm restless, so I take my cloak and my hunting gear and I go out to hunt foxes. I'll be home before midnight.

The stars are out. There is Ursa Major, the Queen of the sky, and Ursa Minor, the cub. That constellation represents us, Her People. The Ursulaic Laws have always been such a big part of our lives; we learnt to read the flowing City Script from it, we learnt our goods and bads, our rights and wrongs, our history and origin and future all from those old, crumbling, crackling pages. Every temple has one book of the Laws, every village, town and city has at least one temple. The capital, Yellowrise, built in sunlight on City Hill, has seven; one for each district. But always, the Bear seemed distant to me. They call Her good. Why? Because She is powerful, feared, respected? So is the king, but he isn't *good*. Treason again. I'll sacrifice in the morning.

For all the rules are drummed into my soul, do I really believe? I've caught two foxes now – by the Bear's grace, or my own skill? An owl hoots and I turn and shoot it. I'm not supposed to shoot owls – they belong to the king – but it's not like anyone will know. Will the Bear know? She doesn't seem to see all Her people starving. I kick the owl when I find it. I don't want to have killed it needlessly- *'be likewise as the Great Bear and act only in thy need'* – but I have no use for it. I put it in my sack and trudge on. How far have I walked? I don't care. As the wood becomes denser, moonlight falls dappled through the half-naked branches. It casts shadows and phantoms into my peripheral vision and makes me skittish. When I hear the heavy footfall of booted feet, I'm already half way up a tree. Sinking into the gnarled bark comes almost as second nature after a childhood of hunting and playing hide-and-seek among these ancient, familiar trees. Below me, two men speak in hushed voices.

'I don't care how hungry I get,' says one man. The other scoffs. 'At least I'll be with my family rather than… practically stealing the food out of their mouths!'

'If we change our minds,' the other warns, 'there'll be no forgiveness from family or crown.'

'I won't change my mind,' the first argues. 'I'd rather have an empty stomach and a clean conscience.'

'We'll both starve,' the second chimes in.

'Doing what's right.'

'Doing what's right.' But they both sound uncertain now. Surely, they're tithe gatherers, separated from their party. I doubt they're trying to catch up with them either. After a silence, the footsteps cease. 'We've made a terrible mistake,' says the second man and the first says nothing. After a few moments, they both take a breath and move on. I listen to them retreat and I stay perfectly still until I can't hear them any more. Then I jump down from the tree and turn north –

the way that the tithe gatherers went. I don't know why; curiosity, maybe. Regardless of motive, I turn, and I walk until I see the cold hint of sunrise and hear the tentative hiccoughs of yawning birds. What am I doing?

## Chapter Two

### Going

I catch up with them around midmorning. They're still lounging round their campfire; the captain is reluctantly packing away his sleeping furs. I stand at a distance among the outskirting trees of the wood. I've never been this far from home. I watch them all, well-dressed, well-fed, laughing, and I hate them.

'Come on then,' the captain calls. 'Pack up, everyone. Time to move on.' There's a round of groans from those still in their sleeping furs. They haven't needed to work since last harvest, perhaps; they look soft and round from inactivity. They all start to gather the donkeys and carts back into formation. Silently, I fall into step with a small man at the rear. 'We need to get home before we eat all the king's tithes!' The captain laughs as he speaks. I hate him. When everyone's ready, we begin to move. I don't have sleeping furs, though my cloak is thick, and I haven't slept. My hunting gear plucks me out of the crowd easily for any observer. After an hour of walking, the small man tells me this.

'I'm coming with you,' I say. He laughs.

'Ask the captain.'

'He can't stop me.' He laughs again. All these people laugh so much. 'He can't,' I insist.

'But he'll want to know you're here. Go forward and walk

with him.' I search the man's face for deceit or ill intent, but he's bleary from sleep and smiling, so I cut round the company and fall into step with the captain. When he sees me, he groans.

'Not another one.' I smile, polite, false.

'Another what, sir?' I hate him.

'We've already taken on one of your villagers. You're so far out on the border, you don't know anything about Yellowrise. I'm sure you must think it's paved with gold!'

'I begin to doubt gold even exists,' I reply dryly.

'Tell your little friend that.'

'Who?' He points. Caught up between two tall men with swords at their hips, laughing and blushing, is Mulberry, the miller's daughter. She's all of fourteen and only just had her first blood. The word around the village is that she's going about with Dunlin, the shepherd lad. A pretty couple to be sure, but he's too sweet for her; she's headstrong and precocious and never takes no for an answer. I'm not surprised to see her here at all, nor to see her hanging off the arms of two handsome men. She, however, seems very surprised to see me.

'Serin?' she gasps, letting go of her smiling new friends.

'Mulberry,' I greet pleasantly.

'What are *you* doing here?' I raise my eyebrows at her. If she wants answers, she'll have to answer too. 'The village was stifling me,' she cries at last, leaning into one of the men and gazing up at him mournfully.

'Mhm.'

'It was! All the boys were boring, silly or young, all the men were taken. I watched them all grow up! How am I supposed to love Dunlin when I remember the time when he was seven and he picked his nose so much in the temple that he made it bleed? You can't make me go back.'

'I'm not here for you.' She frowns at me for a moment.

'But you love the village,' she says slowly, trying to fathom the reason for my presence. I smile at her and say nothing. The men are watching her with laughing eyes. No doubt she'll regret her involvement with them soon enough. They're tithe gatherers; I can't ignore that. All these people chose to help enforce the king's tithes. They're kind in the face and gentle with Mulberry, but they're not good people. They're not to be trusted.

When I go back to the captain, he sighs heavily.

'Still here? Yellowrise isn't the Second Womb, you know.'

The Second Womb. I don't know if I believe in life after death and I certainly don't think Yellowrise is in any way comparable.

'I can work,' I say, instead of dignifying that comment with any sort of response. He sighs again.

'You can hunt, I see. What have you got in that bag, eh?'

'Two foxes,' I reply and his eyebrows go up. Absently, like he's unconscious of the motion, he licks his lips. I wonder if I could sneak the owl I shot into a broth or something? I'd have to be surreptitious. He watches me closely though; I doubt I'd have time.

'For all the food we're carting round,' the captain says, 'and for all we're allowed to draw our rations from it, we never seem to have enough to keep going. It's not fun, you know, driving carts full of food you're not allowed to eat – especially when you're hungry.'

'I help gather the harvests,' I tell him. 'I know.' He sighs again, a great deep sound that expresses some low ache.

'Yes,' he says at last. 'We, all of us, know hunger. The king... The king... Well, what can be said? We all know what the Laws say.'

'*The Great Bear giveth us a Leader,*' I quote, '*and unto this Leader we giveth ourselves.*' The captain looks at me with a dark, thoughtful look. I realise with some surprise that my jaw and my fists are clenched tight. I force myself to relax and shoot him a wan smile.

'Exactly,' he says. 'So what can be done?' He frowns at me as though he might be able to see into my soul. 'We must feed our loved ones,' he continues after a moment, 'and the Bear never seems to hunt for anyone but Herself.'

'Does She not feed Her cubs?' I ask. I know the answer. The captain shakes his head sadly.

'Faith is all we have in the end,' he says, 'when all the food's run out.' I look over at him, some sharp contradiction on my tongue, but he's watching the horizon with a frown and his eyes are glassy. His mouth turns down at the corners in something like a grimace and his feet drag slightly in the dust of the road. I feel for a moment as though I've been shot. Does he go hungry too? Do the tithe gatherers hurt like we do? Do they hate their task? I remember the laughing and the music at the tavern the other night. Did they laugh because they needed to? Did they drink to keep themselves from giving up? I had barely seen them as human, but now I wonder if they feel as I feel, hurt as I hurt, hate as I hate. I put my hand out and place it tentatively on his shoulder. For a few long seconds, he doesn't respond, then he puts his hand over mine and smiles. There's no joy in that smile. Perhaps, and maybe this is more hope than anything, but perhaps, we're not too different. Perhaps he understands.

'Spring will come,' I say after much thought. I barely believe it, but I have to say something.

'What are you doing here?' he asks in return. It's not what I expected and I'm taken off guard.

'I don't know,' I reply. 'I watched you take the tithe, I went out to hunt, and then I realised it was morning and I was here.' It's the truth. He watches me silently for a few long seconds, then sighs again. Why so much sighing? I wonder if he's miserable too.

'I didn't think you the type to just say the truth. I thought I'd have to grapple it from you if I wanted it at all. Thank you for telling me.'

'You believe me?'

'I guess so.' It strikes me as strange that I should have to prove my honesty to a gang of thieves; it isn't *my* integrity that should be under examination. But then, I was holding back out of mistrust, so of course they wouldn't trust me in return. I falter in my stride for a moment as I realise that, to them, I'm a threat. To them, I'm the bad guy. I swallow hard and fall back into step with the captain. I can tell he's still watching me. Why am I here?

'What's our next destination?' I ask in a vain attempt to sound casual and friendly. He shoots me a strange look at that and doesn't answer immediately.

'We've a great many villages of no great importance, then Little Werthing and Greater Werthing. They've built so much between the towns, they're basically one now; I reckon they should call it Greatest Werthing, build a bigger temple and call it a city.'

'How many places do you have to go to? Throughout the whole journey, I mean.'

'Lots,' he replies with a little chuckle. He still doesn't trust me. He glances at my hip dagger whenever it rattles in its scabbard. 'We're only gathering for the western border though, and the south-western corner. We're mostly done now. We'll be back in Yellowrise by next month.'

The moon is waxing. My feet ache as they swing loosely from the cart. The gatherers are lighting a great campfire and I'm trying desperately to keep my eyes open.

'Why did you come?' asks Mulberry, appearing suddenly beside me. She hops up to sit with me and I blink heavily at the crackling beginnings of heat rising up from the sorry pile of sticks.

'I don't know,' I reply quietly. 'I'm just… here. That's all there is to it.' Mulberry watches me through the cold dusk and she opens her mouth a couple of times to speak, before she second guesses herself and falls silent again. 'What is it?' I ask at length.

'You're really not here to bring me back,' she says.

'I didn't even know you'd gone.'

'Oh.' The wood catches and the men give a cheer as they scamper to prepare cooking pots and find their bowls and spoons. They donkeys lie and watch, chewing lazily on grass like lords observing their land, or shepherds watching their sheep. I absently consider that even their donkeys feel entitled.

'Did you want us all to come chasing after you?' I ask.

'I'd have liked at least to have been missed.'

'No doubt they're missing us both, now.' Mulberry leans close to share body warmth and I can feel her hair tickling my ear.

'You always seemed such a quiet, thoughtful person,' she says, soft and tired into the shivering dark. 'You're a lone wolf, a listener. You arrive in silence, say nothing and leave unnoticed. You can be sharp sometimes, some say you can be funny and that you're quick, but I've never heard you raise your voice of speak out or anything. You're always thinking. We all thought you'd be a priestess, not a runaway.'

'I'm not running away,' I contradict, my voice low beneath the hum of fireside conversation. 'I'm following after.'

'After what?' I shrug. 'Destiny? The Bear?'

'I don't know,' I mumble. That phrase is becoming quickly familiar to me. 'Maybe the Bear leads me, because I haven't got a clue. She'd better be leading me, otherwise I'm lost.' Mulberry rests her head on my shoulder and stares up at me through her lashes. We sit for several minutes and then she huffs delicately.

'I feel like I don't know you at all,' she says. 'Like you've been living in the village all these years and I've never really seen you. You're like a ghost or something. Who are you?' I smile slightly, dryly, almost mean.

'I don't know that, either,' I say, my voice harder, and Mulberry draws back in surprise.

'You're here for something,' she whispers, her voice trembling slightly and secretive. 'I know you are.'

'Things happen,' I tell her. The conversation is so hushed

now that she leans forward to hear me better. 'Things happen and there's nothing people like us can do to change it, so we either waste away watching and regretting, or we let it happen, try to keep up, see what'll come of it. I've tried swimming against the tide; it's exhausting. Now I'm letting it sweep me along. Even if it kills me, at least I won't be withered and wasted like-' I snap my mouth shut over that last word. I had no idea I even felt that way.

'Like what?' Mulberry probes and I feel my eyes go hard.

'Like all our parents,' I snap, my voice low still, but stronger. 'Sitting in their chairs, listening to the Laws like it'll make a difference, tutting and sighing and reminiscing but never *doing* anything! Oh, how Mother weeps over the actions of the king! Well, if it matters so much to her, why doesn't she go and… and…'

'Kill him?' suggests Mulberry and my heart thuds hard against my ribcage, my mouth shut over my thoughts, silenced by her words. I laugh then, because there's nothing else I can do, then I stare at her, feeling wild and ragged and cornered.

'Yes,' I say at last, and her eyes widen. 'Why don't we kill him? Why not?' I shake myself, raw and angry, as startled as Mulberry, if not more so, then I slide off the cart and walk away. I'm going to the woods and I'm going to bury the king's owl; I can't use it. I'm not like the Bear at all. *'Act only in thy need.'* What is my need? What's even the point in asking?

My hands are filthy and cold, my knees damp from kneeling as I whispered Rites over the impromptu grave. I feel… empty. It's awful. But as I scamper through dappled moonlight toward the tithe gatherers and their fire, I hear something that makes my toes curl in my boots, my heart ache, my stomach drop. For a moment, I think it's a child screaming and I'm already running by the time I realise it isn't. Something's screaming though, short, horrible shrieks of distress and, as I run, my hand finds the hilt of my hip dagger. I stop abruptly at the edge of a ditch; it's steep and slippery and my heart nearly jumps out of my throat as I stagger and flail for balance. Below me in the sinking dark, I hear the screaming echo.

'Hello,' I call and, for a moment, everything is eerily quiet. Then another stuttered cry comes up and I'm scrambling down through nettles and roots, into dizzying black.

It's to my left, so I reach out, making soft comforting sounds like the ones that nursing mothers make when their child cries at the temple. I push further into the dark and suddenly, I see... something. Two beads of light appear in the gloom and, moments later, my fingertips touch something soft and fluffy. I draw back for a beat, then I reach out again, a wet nose pushes into my palm. A curious tongue touches my wrist, a velvet ear twitches against my arm and I climb up the bank again, feeling claws at my shoulders as the tiny thing clings to my back.

When we reach the top, I sit panting on the ground. It climbs over my shoulder and, in the moonlight, it nuzzles my neck inquisitively.

'Where's your mother, little one?' I ask, and my voice barely lifts above a breath. The cub stares at me and I pet it lightly on the head. Above me, the moon goes out.

How do I describe this? How does it feel? I don't see my life flash before my eyes, I don't feel peaceful or calm or even frightened. It's like my brain just slips away and I'm still. Feelings can wait for later; right now, an angry mother bear towers over me and her cub wriggles in my arms. Silently, I gather it up and place it in the dirt. It immediately bounds happily over to its great protector and she bends down to check on it. When she's sure it's uninjured, she stands again, proud on her hind legs, and stares. I stare back, small and still, holding my breath and waiting. She growls, a low warning rumble, and slumps down to all fours, then she turns and, with her cub in tow, vanishes into the trees. When she's gone, I stand, uselessly dust myself off and turn back towards camp. A few feet away, peeking round a bush, is Mulberry. She stands very still for two, three, four seconds, and then she runs away. I watch her go like I watched the bear: passively. Then I sit down again, and I cry.

When I arrive at the campfire, everything is quiet. An old man with a long beard, probably a travelling priest, is standing on a stool and he's singing a hymn to the Great Bear. It's a song of thanks and of spring. '*The Great Bear rises for the hunt,*' it goes, '*and cubs no more shall cry. Life is blooming, strength returns, no thing shall ever die!*' It's triumphant and hopeful, written by an unnamed bard three hundred odd years ago after the Yellowrise Siege was won by the king. It's a song of victory. The captain stands beside the man on the stool, his dirty cap clutched to his heart. In the arms of one of the large sword-wielding men, Mulberry is curled up with tears in her eyes.

'There,' someone shouts when the song ends and everyone

turns, silhouetted against the huge fire, staring at me, and I freeze like a caught thief, my fingers brushing my hip dagger, my face stone hard and cold. The captain steps forward and bows to me.

'Lady Serin,' he says graciously. 'Come to the fire and warm yourself.' I step forward tentatively and find that all eyes follow me. One young man leaps up and I nearly strike him in my shock.

'I've a tunic you could wear, my Lady,' he says,'so your clothes can be cleaned.'

'Does anyone have spare furs the Lady Serin can use tonight? It's a long way to Yellowrise.' The captain speaks these words, causing immediate commotion. I stand in bewilderment at the fire and the old man offers me his stool to sit on.

'Why?' I ask. 'Have you all gone mad?'

'Lady,' he tells me softly. 'Hide away no longer. The Great Bear chose you and you shall be our salvation. It is written, *when winter weighs heavy on thy shoulders, all ye cubs, wait patiently for spring when the Great Bear shall delivereth up Her people; calleth to thy Mother and Her daughters shall provideth thee thy Sovereign.* What did She tell you?'

'Who?' I ask, distressed and confused.

'The Great Bear,' he replies, animated and eager.

'The Great Bear,' I repeat dully. Mulberry saw me earlier with the cub.

'Yes,' he nods. 'Is She going to deliver us now? Have you received your orders?'

'I need to sleep,' I reply. I absolutely cannot deal with this right now. 'We all need to sleep.' The man bows his head wisely.

'Of course,' he says. 'We'll need our strength tomorrow. We'll need to start recruitment, of course. Yellowrise isn't far enough away to amass an army, but we trust you. She wouldn't lead us astray.' In this moment, mentally and physically exhausted, I can't fathom what he means. Sleeping furs are provided then, so I turn from him and when I've splashed my face and hands with water and changed into a clean tunic, designed for men but comfortable enough, I curl up by the flames and shut my eyes. As I drift, I hear Mulberry nearby, whispering.

'She says she's going to kill the king,' she hisses with reverence. 'The Bear is angry but She's given Her cubs into Serin's arms. By this time next year, the king will be dead. *'The Great Bear killeth when She lusteth after life.'*"

'*Act only in thy need,*' a man's voice agrees. 'And now, we act.'

## Chapter Three

## Arguing

With winter swiftly approaching, it's easy to wake before the sun, but it's hard to get up and out of the warm sleeping furs. When I wake, I find that mostly everyone is already up, working hard to remove the king's banners from the donkeys. I've been woken by Mulberry, I realise slowly, leaning over me with something like awe in her eyes.

'There's a cart you can ride on, if you want to sleep more,' she says, and I'm still so tired, so I do.

When I wake up properly, the sun is shining weakly through thick clouds and we're plodding through fields, sharp with stubble and slick with mud. It must have rained recently; perhaps when I was sleeping. I hug the furs around my shoulders and crawl over to where the driver, a willowy young man, sits singing to his donkey in a low voice. I scramble up to the seat and slump beside him. He glances at me, his song falters for a moment, then he returns to his task and I'm free to think about yesterday.

The bear.

Was that a message from the Great She-Bear? I've never had a message before, or even heard of any human being contacted in such a manner. The Law that the old man recited to me yesterday evening rattles around in my head and I can't make sense of it. Of course, I've heard it before, but I never thought to understand it. *When winter weighs heavy on thy shoulders, all ye cubs, wait patiently for spring when the Great Bear shall delivereth up Her people; calleth to thy Mother and Her daughters shall provideth thee thy Sovereign.* Am I supposed to believe that this Law speaks of me? That the Great Bear was anointing me yesterday while I was burying the body of a needless and lawless kill? While I was cursing Her name and disowning Her in my heart? Is this Her idea of a practical joke? I'm certainly not laughing.

Beside me, the driver retrieves a waterskin and offers it to me. I thank him as I take it and I'm shocked by how raw and sad my voice sounds. All at once, I remember that I nearly died yesterday and I drink more from the skin than I intended to. The man watches me silently. My hands are shaking.

'Thank you,' I say as I pass it back. 'I didn't realise how thirsty I was.'

'You're in shock,' he replies. 'You met the Great Bear last night; of course you're in shock. Rest, Lady. We're almost at the next village.' I don't want to rest any more. I want to talk to Mulberry. I want answers.

'I saw it,' she insists, immediately defensive when she sees how unhappy I am. 'You were sitting with the cub in your lap, then the Great Bear appeared and you were so calm; you just gave Her the cub and you were so collected and she just went without hurting you! She just left!' I put my head in my hands. We're sitting on the edge of a tithe cart as it lumps along. The captain walks a little distance away and I'm pretty sure he's listening.

'Mulberry,' I sigh. She shakes her head.

'You didn't know why you came, you said. And what else did you say? Our parents were complacent. Why not kill the king?'

'If you're so eager, do it yourself. I'm not some prophet or Anointed One.'

'Yes, you are. She anointed you, who knows when, and she commissioned you yesterday. I saw it. I know it.'

'You don't know anything,' I snap, feeling the familiar shudder of anger welling up in my chest. Mulberry stares at me for a few long seconds, then she turns from me. Her shoulders shake slightly; I've made her cry. Finally, she turns back to me and she's got pain and fury in her eyes.

'I know that you were right,' she says, her voice low and trembling. 'We've been too accommodating, too... *obliging*, for too long. The king doesn't know the Bear and the Bear won't protect him any more. I know that much. I know things need to change. Who'll do it if not us? Serin, don't you see? I *know* you're the Bear's Chosen, and even if you're not, does it matter? We need a leader. I'm not a child any more; I know what needs to be done.'

Perhaps she does; her eyes are sharp and angry and, in this moment, she does look old, but I remember when I was fourteen, full of life and hope and dreams.

'You know it'll all come to nothing, right?' Mulberry's anger seems to seep out of her for a beat, confused by the tired hopelessness in my voice, but then she's burning. She turns toward me and lifts her hand. I watch it swing toward me, aiming for my cheek, but I'm a hunter. I'm good, really good, with my bow, and I'm quick. My hand catches her wrist and her eyes widen. We sit in silence, swaying with the motion of the cart for a breath, only a breath, though there's an eternity in it. Beyond our conversation, in the world outside our eyes, somebody shouts. The cart stops with a jolt and I can hear donkeys braying.

'Lady Serin,' gasps the captain, at the edge of the cart, looking up at me with worry between his eyebrows.

'Everything's fine,' I say, my teeth gritted but my tone pleasant.

'No, it's not,' Mulberry snarls. 'Listen to yourself! You're just like them.' In my mind, I see my mother sitting at her spinning wheel with her lone tallow candle, every evening sitting and spinning and staring and slowly wasting away. I see myself beside her, so consumed in watching her rot that I can't see how it's infected me. I drop Mulberry's wrist like it's burnt me and I blink at her stupidly. She glares at me, but the set of her jaw is triumphant.

'I have to go,' I say at length, and I slide off the cart and walk.

Walking is like dancing, and it's the most important part of hunting. Breathe, step, breathe, step, the rhythm of the earth and the thumping of my heart in time with my prey and the trees. The bend of my legs and my bow, the movement of limbs coordinated with the movement of the forest. It's all like dancing and the heartbeats, the footfalls, the noises of the woods, all like music. Not only does it provide food and exercise, it's calming. A meditation, breathing in and breathing out and living entirely in each step, each movement, each sound and sensation. I'm walking now with intent, searching for something, and I can feel the weight of my bow across my shoulders and I breathe. I'm searching for peace, for the back of the party where I can walk alone, and I find myself slipping into the hunter's mindset. My anger and confusion and pain fizzle out; there's no room for things like that on a hunt. I relax my muscles, shake the energy out of my hands and look up. The sky is overcast, the air is clear. Rising up to the west are the Invius Mountains, blue on the horizon and hazy. The world around me moves but the mountains are constant; the view I have of them here is much the same as the one I had at home and we're two days away now. Far above, a buzzard glides on a current of air. Around me, donkeys plod and people talk in low voices or in laughter. Their eyes are bright and I never realised how dark they'd been before. They smile at me or wave as I pass. Were they as hopeless as me? Had we all become as lethargic as Mother, with no fire in her eyes but for her candle, no heartbeat but for the whirring and clicking of the spinning wheel? I can't smile back so I stare at my destination and walk. My dagger bounces against my hip and I can feel the buzz of the earth beneath my feet. I can't breathe. I can't think. I'm just like them. I'm detestable.

We stop for food when the sun reaches its zenith. There's a general sense of excitement in the party and everyone takes more from the tithes than they have leave to. Our lunch, then, is ample and hearty; I have never felt so well fed. As I sit in the grass, staring up at the clouds, Mulberry appears nearby, hovering nervously. She wants to talk.

'What?' I ask at last. She flinches and I suddenly feel horribly guilty.

'I wanted to apologise,' she says quietly.

'Don't be silly,' I reply. My intent was to comfort but it comes out far too harsh. I take a deep breath and try again. She's preparing herself for something. Is she scared of me? 'You have nothing to be sorry for,' I tell her, my voice tight as I swallow my pride. 'Every word you spoke was true. I- Listen, *I'm* sorry. I... shouldn't have... I was wrong.' It's strangely painful to say out loud. I've admitted now; perhaps it will hurt less in the future. Mulberry looks shocked.

'I tried to hit you,' she says. 'I shouted at you. *'Giveth thyself to the Bear's Anointed.'* I was wrong, I was angry-'

'So was I,' I interrupt. People are glancing at us. I pretend not to notice. 'Mulberry, I was trapped in my own mind, so angry at the world that I couldn't see my own faults. What you said to me earlier – it startled me awake. I *needed* to hear that and you're the only one with spine enough to say it.' Mulberry lets out a startled laugh and puts a hand over her mouth.

'To be fair,' she says, her voice weak, 'you were being a bit of an ass.'

'I was being a total ass,' I reply, lowering my voice as though the donkeys might hear us. Mulberry laughs again and I smile behind my hand. 'But Mulberry,' I add and she nods. 'Don't do it again.' Her face goes serious again in an instant. She shakes her head and stammers out a shy promise. I smile at her. It's been a long time since I could smile so easily and, in a moment, she's laughing again. I take a breath, then another and, for one giddy second, I let myself laugh too. It feels... good.

By nightfall, we reach the next village. It looks much the same as mine; full of grey faces and dead eyes. Small children hide behind their mothers' skirts and brazen girls approach with painted smiles in a desperate attempt to earn money. The tithe gatherers leap off their carts and run through the streets and they're singing. Soon, the village is abuzz with it.

'*The Great Bear rises for the hunt and cubs no more shall cry,*' the village calls and Mulberry makes me stand on the back of a cart and smile at people. They stare at me with large, hopeful eyes and parted lips.

'Could it be true?' they whisper. 'Are we saved?' Are they? I daren't suppose that I could save them; I haven't the first clue how. Mulberry is certain that killing the king is the answer, but I don't know. I don't know.

We don't take any tithes here. We sleep in our furs at the tavern and we gather recruits. Recruits. Are we some sort of army now? Several people take supplies and ride back south to my home, spreading the word, they say. I wonder if Mother will care when she hears about this. Will she even stop spinning? Will a light spark in her face? Or is she too far gone in her own sadness? I nearly was myself and I'm still young.

We set out again just before midday the next morning. It will take a week to reach Little Werthing, half a day from there to Greater Werthing and, with all the stopping and starting, something closer to three more weeks until we reach Yellowrise. By the time we get there, I had better have a plan.

# Chapter Four

## Travelling

It turns out that the Werthings are military towns. Because they're quite close to the border still, they're in a tactical location; if Yellowrise were attacked, they could ride over quickly and if the southern border were attacked, they would get there days before the king's army could arrive. Most of the men here can fight and many of the women can handle heavy weaponry. Children with wooden swords strapped to their hips run about in the streets and it seems that the tavern only gets custom because it's situated right next to the smithy. Horses, not donkeys but *actual horses*, whinny at the roadside and eat weeds from among the cobblestones. Cobblestones! Obviously, even Little Werthing solicits more attention from the capital that the other towns on the south-western border.

Everyone is much more shy about showing me off here. Large dark men with leather straps round their forearms guard the huge gates. I've never been to a town with a gate before; I sit in my usual cart with Mulberry, driven by the same willowy man who gave me water, and Mulberry's eyes are shining as she looks the guards up and down.

'Tithe gatherers?' confirms a broad man with long black hair tied into a plait down his back. The captain nods silently. 'The king's little rats,' he spits and signals for the gate to be opened.

'We bring news,' the captain says quickly, failing dismally at hiding his nervousness – and who could blame him? The man squares his huge shoulders and walks right up into the captain's space.

'What?' he growls. 'You're going to gloat before you steal our dinners from out our mouths?'

'We're not taking tithes any more,' the captain replies with false calm. The man's eyebrows shoot up, then he bristles, bustling forward again, herding the captain against the edge of our cart. Mulberry immediately stands and hops over me to jump out onto the dirty cobbles. Through the high wooden poles of the fence, children and young women stare. Mulberry glances at them and flushes pink. She steps up and touches the man's toned arm. He rounds on her in an instant, going still with surprise when he sees her. She smiles coyly at him, tucking a loose strand of hair behind her ear.

'Excuse me,' she says, her voice sweet and high. 'I think you're distressing my Lady.' She gestures to me. I keep my face neutral.

'A noble?' asks the man, looking me over with a mixture of confusion and disgust.

'No,' says Mulberry, her hand sliding curiously over the defined muscles beneath his sleeve. 'She's the Great Bear's, not the king's. She was chosen.'

'Chosen?' The man looks at me closely, the captain forgotten, and I look back, unfazed. Perhaps my lack of fear is what makes him pause. He looks back at Mulberry and places his large hand gently over hers where it rests now on his shoulder. 'By which Law was she anointed?' Mulberry smiles again and steps closer, lowering her voice so he has to lean in to hear her better.

"*Calleth to thy Mother and Her daughters shall provideth thee thy Sovereign.*"

'And what is the calling?'

'The king will die.' The man's hand tightens on Mulberry's for a moment and she gasps, then he puts both hands on her waist and lifts her easily back onto the cart.

'Attend your Lady,' he says, his face shining, though kept professionally straight. He looks to me with a question in his eyes. There's a thousand questions it could be and each has a thousand answers, so I say simply,

'I am Serin.' He bows low and Mulberry pinches my thigh in excitement. 'Who are you?'

'My name is Sorrel. If my Lady seeks my services, I can fight better than most and have the stamina of a horse. I am patient and quick. I would delight in fighting for your cause.'

'I thank you, Sorrel,' I reply. For their sake, I push my shoulders back and sit tall. For Mulberry and the captain and Sorrel – even for Mother. They need a leader, Mulberry said. They need a leader and, for now, I'm all they have. 'I'm more a hunter than a fighter. Diversity will be to our advantage.' I stumble here. He's still watching me, waiting, and I don't know what else to say. 'If I'm to live up to expectation and fulfil the Great She-Bear's will, then I will need people I can trust. I will need people who are strong and resourceful. I will need *you*. Perhaps the Bear trained you for this very time. I will welcome you if you offer.' I hold my hand out to him and he grasps it with reverence. 'Welcome, brother,' I say and he smiles, just for a moment, then he springs back and starts calling.

'Open the gates, open the gates! The Bear hath provided us our Sovereign!' The gates swing open and we tether our donkeys and carts in the square. It seems the whole of Little Werthing has come out to meet us. Mulberry helps me down from the cart and she's grinning at me like a madwoman.

'Thank you,' she whispers as I sling my hunting sack over my shoulder. I offer her a thin smile and we head to the tavern; I need a drink. Perhaps the Bear isn't as distant as I thought, because every person in the tithe gathering party gets good ale on the house. By the time night falls, I've told and retold a careful version of my bear cub story, without mention of killing the king's owl, a hundred times over and, when I'm offered a room, I fall into the bed and sleep like the dead. When I rise, I have an army at my disposal and when we troop off for Greater Werthing, Little Werthing is left silent and empty. Now, it seems, we have begun.

Greater Werthing, much like Little Werthing, is a blur of noise and introductions to me. It's less military for the sole reason that it's larger and therefore has a greater population, but it's still got soldiers on every street corner. We spend two days there and I barely see more of it than the square, where I stand with Mulberry, nodding at people uncomfortably while she tells my story. She embellishes it and draws it out with much gesticulation and many a dramatic pause. I thought that people would lose faith in me when they heard even the modified story of the bear and the cub, but it seems to have fuelled them on. Mulberry's getting more out of this than I am; she's flushed and animated, shaking hands and calling people over to talk to them. Standing just behind us is

Sorrel with his hand hovering over his sword. His bright eyes dance about as he waits and watches, keeping guard over us. Every time Mulberry clasps someone's hands in greeting, he grimaces.

We set out early on the morning of the third day. We've grown now to a large entourage. Women with daggers and arrows sit in the carts, armoured men on horseback go ahead and behind. When we stop for the night, people gather together and put up tents. These are all provisions kept for times of war and they're being used in joy and peace, simply in order to bring comfort to us all.

The nights are steadily getting colder now that we're approaching the wrong end of September. Above us as we travel, the sky slowly grows darker and lower; rain is on the way. And as we move, the Invius Mountains spread their shadow over us, oppressive or protective, I can't tell, but it comforts me. On a plateau in the foothills, the king's winter retreat is sheltered from the worst of the weather. He will head west with a company of servants and nobles and with his personal Guard come mid-October. We'll arrive by the first of the month, if we make good time. We'll only have a few weeks to work in and I still have no idea how we'll achieve what we work towards. Besides, how comfortable do I really feel about killing a man? A foul, evil man, to be sure, but a living, breathing person with a family. Will his son take the throne right away? Will he be any better than his father? Will we all be put to death for treason?

Every minute feels like a day and every week feels like a second. I'm in turmoil and I speak to no one. Sorrel travels alongside us; Mulberry flirts with him shamelessly and rides in front of him on his saddle for hours each day. He smiles at her and I come to realise that, until now, I'd never known true isolation. At home, I'd felt lonely. I felt like nobody cared at all and I was angry and bitter. I didn't want company because I didn't like the people around me. Now, with a cooling temper, a strange fondness for my companions and a plethora of troubles and emotions I desperately want to let out, I feel totally, absolutely, overwhelmingly alone. I long for the woods and the rhythm of the hunt. I yearn for the familiar hoot of the king's owls and the whisper of leaves. It was good to be alone then and I revelled in it. Now, it's a cage.

Mulberry smiles at me and waves, leaning her head back against Sorrel's collar. I lift my hand in acknowledgement and return to sharpening sticks into arrows. It is written, *when a cub hungereth, it calleth to its mother. When a cub feareth, it calleth to its mother. When a cub resteth, it resteth with its mother. Worry not, ye cubs, but calleth to thy Mother and the Great Bear shall cometh to thy aid.* In desperation, I mutter my woes into my sleeping furs at night. When I sleep, I never dream. I am alone.

The yellow-walled fields and orchards are the first sign that we're approaching the city. We start seeing farmers and farmhands, then shepherds with sheep or goats, fields of cattle and tiny rows of cottages. The rich farmland that surrounds Yellowrise sits almost in a perfect circle in a valley of sorts beneath City Hill. On the flat top of that hill is the city, built in the distinctive local stone, casting its arm of influence, fear and literal shadow over the outskirting villages. We pass through Crossroads, a miniscule settlement with little more than an inn with large stables. Most of the customers are travellers, merchants and pilgrims and the women gathered at the well outside sneer at us as we pass. A couple of men on horseback stop to talk to them, to tell them the good news.

'Have you heard?' I hear them say as my cart lumps past. 'The Lady Serin of the Great Bear has risen up to fulfil the Laws! She is the Anointed and we'll all presently be set free by her hand.' I feel small in a dark tunic I borrowed from a man. I shrink into it and hide in my cloak. I bow my head and dream of the mountains.

# Chapter Five

## Advising

When we reach the main gate, a large number of soldiers are waiting for us. We stop at a distance and the captain moves forward to speak with them. When he returns, he's pale-faced.

'Word has come to Yellowrise that a rebel army come to kill the king. We have been denied access to the city, the soldiers threaten us with arrest if we don't go home and the king has retreated early to the Invius Plateau.' Word spreads throughout the group and we turn back to Crossroads, settling quietly down at tables at the inn. The innkeeper watches us with small, glittering eyes. Every face is turned to me. I take a breath and stand.

'Firstly,' I begin, and there's an unsettling hush as everyone strains to hear. At the door, a man's voice repeats the word to those who couldn't fit inside. 'I want to remind everyone that this... *mission* we're on is not ours, but the Great Bear's.' There's a general round of agreement and nodding from all who listen. I swallow hard and continue. Surprisingly, my voice doesn't shake; the rest of me does. 'Secondly, I want to remind you that this isn't something we're doing because we want to. We're doing this because it's the right thing to do, and therefore the *only* thing to do.' There's a small cheer then. Outside, people bellow and whoop. 'Thirdly, I want to remind you that, though I have been selected as leader, we are all the Bear's people, Her cubs, and therefore have a say in how we continue from here. I *remind* rather than *tell* you these things because you already know them. You are all good people.' A cheer. 'Strong people!' Another cheer. 'Resilient, powerful, worthy people!' I feel a little giddy, a little sick. The innkeeper stares at me with his pinprick eyes and beside me, Mulberry keeps whispering encouragement. 'We are brothers and sisters, equals in the Bear's eyes, and we do this together. We live together, fight together, die together, hope together. We dream one dream!' My audience seem to love what I'm saying. A heady cry rises, a chant of my name and I clutch the edge of the table, my fingertips white with the pressure, just to keep myself standing. 'I want-' I say, but everyone's shouting still. I glance down desperately to Mulberry and she springs up immediately, holding her arms up. After a moment, everything falls silent and still. 'I want to do this properly. I want to do this well. I want to show you that you have made the right decision, putting your trust in me as we follow the Bear. In order for that to happen, I need to hear what you have to say. I will appoint ten people to be your voice; go to them, speak to them, tell them what you want, what you fear, what you are willing to do for our cause. They will report to me. Understand your power, friends; each one of you is my personal advisor. We must try to make a decision by tomorrow. If you want to go home, do. We need passion now. We need hearts of fire and wills of iron. If you are uncertain, this is not your calling. Hear me! Listen, and I will lead you in the manner that you follow me.' I'm not sure that made any sense at all. I feel in equal measures that I said too much and not enough. I slump down, boneless, into my chair and Mulberry supplies me with a pint of water. I drink it quickly then I turn to Sorrel, who sits opposite us. 'You know many of these people. Gather eight who you trust and who listen well. You and Mulberry make up the ten. I... I need to sacrifice.'

'I'll call someone to ride you to the next village; there's a temple there.'

'Thank you, Sorrel,' I say and Mulberry gives me another pint. Within five minutes, I'm being led through the bustling crowd to a horse and I'm shaking still and the thud of galloping hooves and the unfamiliar bounce in the saddle keep my mind occupied until I'm being guided by the arm into a tiny building that smells of smoke and dust. On a low alter against the icon-covered back wall is the local copy of the Ursulaic Laws. Coming toward us is an old man in the priest's hood. I go up to the alter and kneel shakily. The rider who brought me sits down in a pew and the priest returns to his lectern where he is probably composing his High Day speech. What day is it? It feels like an eternity since I went to temple. I put my hand out toward the book of Laws and I press my forehead against the floor to pray. I do this so rarely and I've *never* prostrated myself before. I've seen others do it when they make a big sacrifice or when a loved one is dying. I think the priest is watching me but, in this moment, I really don't care. I hear rain suddenly start to fall outside and it feels miles away. Like the criminals who sacrifice for forgiveness and the mothers praying for their newborns, I stretch myself out at the alter and wail, low in my throat. I tremble and cry because I can't stop it and I don't fully know why and I wail my wordless lament to the Mother Bear. I do this until my tears run dry and my throat closes up. I do this until I'm exhausted and I can't do it any more. Then I sit back on my heels and look up at the pictures on the walls. The first one to catch my eye is the Great Bear standing on Her hind legs, huge paws outstretched in fury, jaws wide and eyes wider as She lusteth after life and I remember the owl. *Act only in thy need,*' I think and it rattles round in my head. What do I need? What do all those people need? What does the Bear want of me, if She wants me at all? I slump back onto my rump and hunch over, staring at the floor, but after a time, I become aware of someone standing behind me. I straighten up slowly and turn my head. At my shoulder is the beady-eyed innkeeper from Crossroads. He's damp from the rain and watching me intently and seems pleased to see my tear-stained face, no doubt red and puffy too.

'Lady Serin,' he says in a low, smooth voice.

'Can I help you?' I ask.

'I was hoping I could help you,' he replies and his tiny eyes look out at me as though he truly sees me – all of me – and I feel exposed somehow, until I see a kindness in the curve of his mouth.

'How can you help me?' I sigh unhappily. 'I've been thrown in miles from shore and I'm drowning.'

'You never learnt to swim then,' he says solemnly and kneels down beside me. 'But you're surrounded by people who did, who can, who are.' I look up at him quizzically and he supplies me with a cloth to dry my eyes with. 'I liked what you said earlier,' he tells me at last. 'Telling them all to advise you, putting people in place to hear their thoughts. You knew you couldn't do it so you gave the task to someone who could.'

'I don't know if I can do anything,' I reply and it feels so good to be telling someone, as though it's some dirty secret and letting it out equates to letting it go.

'You can spin a good speech,' he nudges my arm companionably, 'and you can delegate. You have an army, so why are you fighting alone?'

'I don't know what I'm doing.'

'You don't need to, you just need to coordinate what everyone else is doing. Person One is cutting vegetables, Person Two is boiling meat. Now make sure that all the food is ready in time for the meal. That's all there is to it.' I look up at him, startled and confused.

'Can I trust you?' I ask, almost timid in my anxiety.

'I'm not asking you to,' he replies with a quick smile. 'I'm asking you to trust yourself, or if not yourself then your friends. They can trust you if you can't; you just need to trust them.'

'I don't-'

'Think about it,' he interrupts. 'Just think. Think about what you said earlier. Your followers will tell you what to do; the Bear will show you how.' He glances over his shoulder then, a brief, furtive look, before he sniffs and stands up.

'Why help me?' I ask him, somewhat desperately. He winks at me and pinches his handkerchief back from my hands.

'Because you're right. We're all brothers and sisters. We live, hope and die together. We dream one dream and it's freedom. If you really listened, Serin, nobody would ever be able to tell you anything you didn't already know. Now, go; you're needed.' He stuffs the damp cloth into his trouser pocket, turns smartly on his heels and walks out. For a long time, I sit thinking, then I stand on weak legs and turn to go. By the door, the priest and my rider talk together in low voices about the uprising. When I arrive, they say their goodbyes and we ride in silence back to Crossroads. The fresh hoof prints in the wet road are the only evidence that the innkeeper had been there. When we get back, his wife meets us and shows me to a bedroom where I gather my ten advisors. They talk, debate, argue together late into the night, and I sit, drying my rain-wet hair, and I listen.

When the sun rises behind thick clouds, it's still raining.

'It's an omen,' the willowy driver of our cart says to Mulberry, voice hushed as we prepare the donkeys for travel. Most of our number remain at Yellowrise in order to spread the word, gain support, disguise our departure and prepare the city for a new monarch. Who? The prince? Me? Please not me.

A select number of us, fifteen to be precise, are travelling to the Invius Plateau. The party voted quickly for a new set of leaders in my absence – several of the advisors I appointed yesterday, the captain and a few others to work as a sort of council for anyone at the city. Mulberry, Sorrel, a number of soldiers from Little Werthing and a few women are joining me. The captain, though he was appointed by the people, is reluctant to stay behind. Now, he stands in the doorway of the Crossroads inn, watching us load provisions and tents onto the carts. We'll move faster in a small group, as well as drawing less attention. Still, there are more of us than I'd have liked, though fewer than will perhaps be necessary; none of us have any idea what the Plateau is like and therefore how to prepare for it. We set off at about midday. I don't see the innkeeper.

Mulberry seems to be in high spirits at least, though everyone else seems quite downcast. Postponing the conflict surely was good; we had no plan and even less chance at succeeding at anything we may have decided to try. It's a relief to me; to everyone else, it's a failure. As we slip back into the rhythm of travel, I huddle up into myself and go quiet.

Days pass, only days, before Mulberry's had enough of watching me withdraw.

'You don't want to be here,' she tells me one night as we lie in the back of a hooded cart, shivering in our sleeping furs.

'Why do you say that?' I reply, and find that my voice is rough from disuse.

'You just mope all day. You don't even sit with me, but you walk along behind us and stare ahead like you're sleepwalking.'

'I've always wanted to go to the Invius Mountains,' I muse. 'Now I'm actually going and it's to-' I cut myself off quickly. It's to kill a man. I can't say that to Mulberry. I blink as I remember that she's just a child still.

'You don't want to be here,' she repeats. 'You don't want to do this.' I remember my speech at Crossroads – *'If you are uncertain, this is not your calling'* – and I feel like such a hypocrite.

'Does it matter?' I hiss back guiltily. 'I have to, so I will. Why does it matter how I feel about it?' Mulberry says nothing for a long time and I start to wonder if she's fallen asleep, but then she rolls over to face me in the dark.

'Why don't you want to?' she asks and she sounds breathless.

'For the Bear's sake, Mulberry,' I gasp. 'Hasn't it occurred to you that we're planning a murder?' I put a cold hand over my mouth as though to silence the words that I've already let loose. Beside me, Mulberry draws in a sharp breath through her teeth.

'If we don't, he'll never stop,' she says at last. 'We'll just have to wait for him to hibernate. He's not *young*; it can't be that long…'

'Yes,' I reply. 'Hibernate with the Bear and all his ancestors, resting like a king rather than rotting like a criminal – which is what we'll do. You know, being murderers.'

'But *'the Great Bear killeth when She lusteth after life'*. Serin, *we* lust after life!'

'I'm going through with it, Mulberry; you don't need to convince me. I'm just a bit *emotionally* conflicted – nothing to worry about.' Again, Mulberry goes quiet. I can feel her eyes watching me through the shadows of the night.

'At least spend time with us as we travel,' she pleads. 'If you close in on yourself, you'll go right back to anger and inaction. It was so lovely, watching you open up and rise to your calling. Please don't sink back down now; we need you.' I remember what the innkeeper at Crossroads told me: *'your followers will tell you what to do; the Bear will show you how.'*

'For you, Mulberry,' I say slowly. 'For your sake, I won't go quiet. When this is all over, I'm going somewhere alone where I can be silent without interruption. If you need me to be present then I will be. It's all I can do, I suppose.'

'You're a naturally quiet person,' she observes. 'That's fine. But we need you to speak up for us.'

'I understand.'

'Thank you.' She rolls away again and I presently hear her breathing even out in sleep. I lie awake and stare at the leather hood, listening to the rain beat against it, and I pretend that this is a hunt. The king's a fox; it's not a needless death. Months ago now, I lay awake dreaming of the Great Bear tearing a tavern to shreds. I was so angry, so bitter. Now, I picture Her paw sweeping a single deadly blow. There's no anger, no passion, hardly any feeling at all, but the rush of blood, the pang of necessity, the thud of finality. After that, I breathe like I've just found out how. I sink down from my hind legs and sniff the body cautiously; there's no movement. I live.

# Chapter Six

## Uniting

I start talking to the people I travel with. I hear what it was like growing up in Little Werthing, I listen to the pains of a bereaved mother, I learn how to make a hoard of different meals out of one fox. At home, we had ways of spicing the dish or adding different things to parody diversity. On the road, there's not even that, but these women have their ways and every night, the stew tastes wonderful. They smile and laugh and bicker and show me their secrets and I join in. It feels strange; good, almost. They're kind and I find myself loving them. The men try teaching me how to sword fight and I try to teach them how to hunt, but we're too impatient as students and too lenient as teachers. In a blur of laughter and singing, eating together and trying desperately to keep warm, weeks pass. Ahead of us, the mountains grow steadily larger.

At mid-afternoon one day, as I'm napping on the front of my cart with my head in the driver's lap, I hear Mulberry laugh from nearby. Cracking an eye open, I see Sorrel's mare coming up beside us. For a moment, I make eye contact with the driver above me, then I shut my eyes again. Quietly, I hear him huff in amusement.

'Why did you leave?' Sorrel asks jovially. Mulberry sighs

dramatically but there's a smile in it.

'It was stifling in the village! We're so close to the border, we barely see *anyone* else – even from the next village. Our parents are all old and boring, stewing in their own tears, yet not willing to work for change. They remember the last king, you see, so they're far too invested in the letter of the Law – *'the Great Bear giveth us a Leader–'*

*'And unto this Leader we giveth ourselves,'* Sorrel finishes for her. She hums and she sounds content, somehow. 'Do you know how old I am?' he asks now. 'Am I old and boring? If I'd started young, I could have fathered you.'

'I'm fourteen,' Mulberry gasps, sounding scandalised. 'I'm not some infant; I don't need fathering. Besides, you can't be older than...' she trails off as she tries to guess.

'I'm thirty,' he tells her after the pause goes on a little too long and she screams and laughs.

'You're not!'

'I am!' They squabble lightly. I feel, rather than hear the driver laughing at them. 'So you didn't like your elders and that's why you ran away?' Sorrel asks finally, drawing the conversation back on track.

'Partly,' Mulberry giggles. 'Also, I felt suffocated. There was no adventure, no romance, nothing for a girl to do.'

'So you left in order to flirt.'

'In order to *love*,' she corrects.

'And have you?'

'I've done an awful lot more since leaving than I could possibly have foreseen, but I've done a bit of falling in love here and there.' There's a coyness in her voice as she says this and I realise that I'm being exposed to flirtation. I myself have never done much flirting, despite being closer to Sorrel's age than Mulberry's. I'm not sorry for that; I don't really understand why Mulberry likes doing it so much.

'Only a little?' Sorrel teases her. She laughs, light and easy and, for a moment, I envy her for that.

'If that's all I'm willing to say then it ought to be enough for you. But how about you? You came to fight and there's been no fighting.'

'No,' Sorrel agrees smilingly, 'so I followed your example and did a bit of falling in love. Only a *little* bit,' he clarifies when she starts to laugh again. They're teasing each other, I think. It seems pointless and silly to me to dance around something when you could just step forward and have it. But, I suppose, I've always been a simple person; all I ever wanted was a full stomach and a quiet night. Above me, the driver is laughing again, quietly. He leans down a little and whispers to me.

'She's turned around in the saddle to whisper in his ear. Oh! Now he kisses her. Sickening, isn't it?' I grin and open one eye to look up at him.

'Disgusting,' I agree and he lets out a bark of laughter loud enough to disturb the romancing couple.

'Is she awake?' Mulberry calls and the driver falls silent, still shaking with concealed mirth. I sit up and rub my eyes theatrically.

'I'd be sleeping still if you hadn't been so loudly declaring love right next to me.' She disregards this with a wave of her hand and smiles carelessly. Sorrel has a hand resting on her waist and is watching her with quiet, happy eyes. I wonder how this will all end for them. I wonder if they will have any sort of ending to be glad of. I spring off the cart; I need to walk for a while, because I can't see an ending for any of us where we aren't all dead. Not long now; the mountains grow almost as quickly as the cold. Please, I pray in my heart, please let me die just as quickly, or not at all. Being such a small company has definitely kept us hidden for a time, but the king must know by now that we're on our way. When I sleep these nights, that is my prayer; let me die quickly or not at all. But for the love of all, please give Mulberry her happy ending!

It turns out that the Invius Plateau is accessible by one long and narrow road through the foothills of the mountains. It's sheltered entirely on three sides, the majority of the castle built into the rock face, windows facing south-east to catch both the sun and a view of distant Yellowrise, glistening gently among the swirling mass of farmland. I've never the seen the view, but even from the foothills I begin to understand what it must be like. We can only catch glimpses of the Plateau from down here, our vision mostly filled with the looming grey mass of stone, more formidable than exciting, up close. It seems cruel to me that my childhood dream of coming here should be fulfilled in a manner so sure to kill me. At least I'll die with no regrets.

There's nowhere to hide on the approach, so we walk up to the lower gates like guests knocking on the door. There's no other way of doing it and, as such, we're met at the gate by a troop of soldiers. Above us, archers bend their bows and stare us down. They herd us like sheep so we're surrounded and then they chain us into a line and drag us to a cold prison.

Fifteen of us, men and women, with our weapons confiscated and our wrists bound together, sitting in a row, huddled for warmth, praying.

'What now?' Mulberry asks into the darkness. Someone is crying.

'Patience,' I reply. 'We're too far gone to stop now.'

'They're stronger than us,' somebody argues and I click my tongue like the Wise Women mixing their medicines. *No respect*, they'd croak. *Young folk these days wouldn't know wisdom if it were spoon-fed to 'em – which it is! Pah!* And some would spit on the ground and curse and we'd run away shouting and laughing and they'd be laughing too.

'Never corner a wounded animal,' I say now. 'They may be stronger but we've got nothing to lose.'

'Except our lives.'

'What's life in a prison while our families starve?' I shoot back, my voice hard as it echoes off the icy walls. It's the last word; nobody speaks after that.

A man comes with a tray to feed us, who knows how long after we arrive. There's barely enough to go around. He smiles nastily as he sets it down and I realise that he's waiting for us to fight for it.

'Who wants the bread?' I ask immediately.

'I ate shortly before we arrived,' somebody speaks up, 'so I'll pass today.'

'I'll just have broth, thank you.'

'Mulberry's the youngest; give it to her.'

'No, no, Mother Siskin's the oldest; give it to her.' The man's eyes grow wide as he watches us calmly share the food, give our thanksgivings to the Great Bear and eat together. There's no fighting; nobody even glares. When he's taken away the bowls, we sing songs together until we're told severely to shut up by a hoarse shout from outside. Then we sit in silence, each to their own thoughts and, for a week perhaps, then two, then however many lifetimes more, we exist as an entity, united in our dreadful hope and fear, and nobody says a word.

# Chapter Seven

## Escaping

One night, we can hear music and dancing from the castle above us.

'What's the occasion?' I ask the sneering guard when he brings in our dinner.

'It's Solstice,' he replies grimly.

'Ah,' gasps Mulberry, 'can I make a special Solstice request?' The guard turns and stares at her, waiting to hear what she wants. 'May I be moved two spaces to my left?' There's a long pause, then the guard shrugs his shoulders, turns and leaves. A few minutes later, he returns with two other guards and Mulberry is moved. When they leave, she leans into Sorrel with a sigh and he kisses the top of her head.

The next day, the music continues.

'I don't care how it's *usually* done,' someone says, voice hard and even, projected though not raised – the voice of a leader. Everyone sits up straighter and listens. 'Today, I will do it. You do as I command; don't forget your place.' There's a scuffling beyond the door, then the guard opens it, stepping aside feverishly for another to enter.

He's young, about my own age, and tall, as pale as ice and just as cold. He barely looks at the guard as he carries in our food tray. His broad shoulders are pushed back, his thin lips set in a line. His rich silk tunic hangs from his muscular frame in blues and pearls and silver clasps. His boots click on the stone floor. His pale blue eyes match his robes and identify him – they run in his family. He sets the tray down before us and I move forward to share it out as usual, everyone else struck into inaction by his presence. He clicks his fingers and the guard brings a chair before leaving hurriedly.

'Will you be eating with us this evening, Your Highness?' I ask pleasantly. He looks at me with his cool eyes and quirks an eyebrow. After a moment, he shakes his head. 'Of course,' I say, hiding my nerves behind manners and courtesy, 'there must be a feast upstairs. How silly of me.'

'My father will eat most of it,' the prince replies with so much scorn in his voice it makes me pause. He laughs then, not happily, and leans back in the chair. 'They say you are the most civil and generous prisoners we've ever had,' he tells me. 'I wanted to see for myself and look! You share the food so easily.'

'We are all well accustomed to hunger, my Lord,' I say, voice low, and he nods gravely, pressing his lips together so tightly they go white.

'I am aware,' he replies at last. 'But here, I am at a disadvantage. You know who I am, but I don't know you. They say you are assassins.'

'Have we killed?' I ask. 'We are not assassins.'

'Then who are you? My men say that a great she-bear has been standing by the lower gates this past month, just staring. It arrived just after you did, so; which man here leads your little party?' There's an awkward silence that stretches on for just a little too long. I look over to Mulberry for assistance and she immediately jumps into action.

'Your Highness,' she says, 'I humbly present to you, my mistress, Lady Serin, anointed by the Bear, appointed by the people, leader of the uprising and Daughter of the Great Mother.' I flush at such an introduction and bow my head. To my surprise, everyone has lifted themselves up a little and look to me with something like pride in their faces. The prince leans forward in his chair and, for a long moment, we hold eye contact. He has a look about him like he's used to people being unable to look for long, but I find that I'm not afraid of him. He seems impressed by this and looks over at my people.

'My father the king is the Bear's Anointed,' he tells Mulberry. She shakes her head and his eyebrow quirks again.

'Not anymore, Sire. She withdrew Her blessing when he abused Her cubs. Lady Serin saved Her cub and has therefore been chosen.'

'I was chosen to lead a rebellion,' I put in here, 'not to take the throne. We aim to end the king's reign, not his family. So long as you love the Bear, my Lord, you have nothing to fear from us.'

'*I*, fear *you*?' he asks, a bark of laughter rising from his chest, still with no humour or joy at all. 'I promise I shan't do *that*. But you might fear me.'

'No, Sire,' I say. '*I* do not fear you. You seem too much like myself; too full of anger and bitterness at injustice to see that you aren't alone in it.' He stares at me then, like he can't believe what he's hearing. At last, he licks his lips and leans even farther forward.

'The Great She-Bear anointed you?' he asks, almost in a

whisper. 'You are certain?'

'We are certain,' Mulberry says quickly, her voice strong. 'I saw it happen. She has lead us well.' The prince leans back now and observes Mulberry with a curious eye.

'You're a vivacious young thing,' he says. 'Full of life and spirit. You're very sure of your Lady, aren't you. Are you as sure of yourself?' Beside her, Sorrel's lip curls back in warning; I can see him shaking. Mulberry bats her eyes, however, and blushes.

'Sire,' she breaths and it's exactly the coy tone she used on Sorrel when they laughed together on the road. Beside her, Sorrel goes very, very still.

'Guard,' the prince calls suddenly. 'I'm leaving now, and I'm taking that one with me.' The guard unchains Mulberry and binds Sorrel to the man who sits on her other side. She stands and takes the arm offered to her. She looks up at him with big eyes and smiles; she doesn't look back. For the first time in months, I feel a surge of anger rise like bile in my chest, but it's beaten back down when I hear Sorrel. He lets out a low moan, like he's been stabbed. For a long time, he laments and then we all sit in silence. Where the guard failed to tear us apart, Mulberry has succeeded; everyone turns away from their neighbour. Sorrel refuses comfort so we cease to offer it. It is now that I realise that I have never been their leader; I have only ever been Mulberry's spokesperson. Our true leader is gone. She has left us. What now?

The party upstairs lasts for a full week. The day after it ends, a soldier in rich green robes arrives and quietly gathers us up.

'The prince has graciously called for your release,' he tells us. 'Now we must get you out of the castle before the king finds out.' He smiles grimly and leads us, still in chains, to a door in a high tower. There, we are unbound, given back our weapons and equipment with three sturdy pack ponies and a large supply of food, then ushered out into an icy stone pit. A narrow path running up the side is the only clue as to any kind of activity here at all; even the door seems reluctant to swing on its hinges. 'Follow that path,' the soldier says. 'The mountain goats made it for you. It will bring you to a lake and a cabin; a fire will be waiting for you there, and beds. Go quickly. Don't leave there until we tell you to.' We take the ponies and we go.

Though the way is steep and slippery, treacherous in places and openly malicious in others, we make it to our destination before sundown. A fire is indeed waiting in a large log cabin. The women silently cook us dinner. We're only feeding fourteen now. Fourteen. That's far too young; she should never have come.

Sorrel refuses to eat. His muscles have softened after a month on a prison floor and he lays in one of the little straw cots and speaks to no one.

'Something has happened, is happening, is about to happen,' I tell everyone after dinner. 'We can't lose hope. The prince knows the king's cruelty no doubt better than anyone.'

'He is the same as his father,' a woman says, voice low, and I resist the urge to curl up and block everything out.

'He's the only chance we have. He has been kind in all but one respect.'

'But it's the one that matters most.'

'Let the Bear worry about that; all we need to worry about right now is not dying. Everything else will come together.' Where have my words gone? I'm useless without Mulberry urging me on.

'Don't you care?' a man demands of me. In this moment, I can't remember his name, though we hunted and sang together only last month. I stare at him, my eyes dark.

'Do not speak with haste,' I tell him sharply. 'Disunity will be our undoing. Didn't you hear the prince? The Great Bear doesn't hibernate; she waits for us outside.'

'You didn't answer my question.'

'That's because it's foolish,' I reply. 'Would I be here if I didn't care? We have all given so much! I-' I stop short here. What can I say? There's nothing to be said. I slump down into a chair. All eyes are on me. 'Do you respect me?' I ask. Everyone exchanges quiet looks, then they slowly nod. 'Would you respect me any less if I were to have a little cry quickly?' Again, they seem to consult one another before they all shake their heads. I let out a breath, thank them, drop my head into my hands and let go. As I cry, it feels awful, but when I'm done, I feel better. Nobody speaks to me, so I wrap a cloak around me and go out to the lake. It's iced over but it's not frozen through. I take a bucket with me and return with water that we boil and drink hot.

Sorrel hasn't moved since we arrived. In one go, we have lost two vital members of our group. We band together as best we can, singing, praying, talking, working in harmony as we wait. Sorrel is as good as dead. Now, more than ever, I must live.

## Chapter Eight

### Waiting

I've never really thought about what living entails. What do I do? How do I act? What even is life? There's one in our number, old Mother Siskin, who has been smiling ever since we arrived, so I turn to her for advice. She's probably the oldest person I've ever seen but she still seems sprightly; she came due to popular demand rather than practicality and insists she's here as spiritual and moral support. When I sit down beside her at the table where she's kneading dough with enough vigour to put her younger helpers to shame, she beams wide enough that I could count how many teeth she's missing, if I wanted to.

'Serin, dear,' she warbles. She's never addressed me as Lady and probably never will. 'Move your chair over a little; I can't see you properly from this angle.' I shift obediently. 'You came to me in order to listen, so sit quiet for a bit and let me tell you a story.' I nod. Mother Siskin is cheerful and friendly but she brooks no opposition. 'When I was born, the king's grandfather was on the throne,' she begins in her shaking, powerful voice. 'My mother died in childbirth when I was four and I raised my little sister in destitution for a few years.'

'Oh my,' I say sympathetically, but she's still smiling.

'When I was seven, my sister and I came to Greater Werthing. I took her to the temple on the High Day and stopped to talk with the priest afterwards. He was impressed by my faith and my reasoning, and by my knowledge of the Laws, since we had taken shelter in temples more often than not over the years. He took me on as a student and trained me to be a priestess. When my sister was old enough to work, I took the rites and became a priestess just a few months before my mentor passed on. I served in Greater Werthing for fifty years. All throughout my service, I studied medicine and healing, so when I retired, I took up witchcraft and became a Wise Woman. All my life, I taught my congregation to make their own interpretation of the Laws and I told them to be angry about injustice. When you arrived, my people were primed to become your people. When you brought us here, I knew I had to come. My life has been long and fulfilling; it won't last much longer.'

'You're dying?' I ask in shock and she laughs.

'Dying is little more than the next step. There's pre-life, life and post-life; I am quite content with this. Now tell me, what did you want to ask?' I don't understand why she's told me all this and I take a moment to digest it before I reply. She pauses her kneading in order to watch me think and she seems pleased with me.

'I was wondering why you're always happy,' I confess at last and she throws her head back to laugh in glee.

'I'm not,' she says simply.

'What?' She steps away from her dough and another woman takes over for her. She sits down beside me and places a floury hand on my knee.

'I am happy when things are good and sad when things are bad. Feeling bad is a healthy reaction to bad situations; it motivates us. But I'm never without hope or without gladness. Those things are much more steadfast than the ebb and flow of emotion.'

'How do you cultivate them? Tell me, Mother Siskin, how do I lead these people when we're all miserable?' She clicks her tongue at me now.

'Girl, you're not listening.' I remember suddenly the innkeeper in Crossroads. *'If you really listened, Serin, nobody would ever be able to tell you anything you didn't already know.'* Mother Siskin is watching me like she knows my mind.

'Help me,' I say at last and she grins again.

'Walk with me,' she says and I'm more than glad to do that.

We walk up a steep mountain path to the woods that cloak the rim of our little valley. The goats watch us curiously but they don't know humans well enough to run away. We're part of nature here, padding along soundlessly in fur boots. We find a small cave and light a fire there. We sit down and watch the flames and Mother Siskin closes her eyes.

She grew up in poverty – not just a peasant like me, but homeless, an orphan, raising her little sister from infancy. Where was hope and gladness there? Where was hope for me when my father died? Where was gladness as I watched my mother wilt like autumn? I can feel that old familiar fury in my gut and I grit my teeth and glare at the flames. Mother Siskin opens one eye and nods at me and I feel released from some dreadful silence. I scream then, at the fire, at the mountains, at the Bear, at Mother Siskin, at myself. I roar and scratch the ground beneath my knees until my nails are torn and bloody. Then I sob aloud. Finally, I feel sated. I sit back and stare at the fire again; it crackles on, undisturbed and all my theatrics feel totally insignificant. I still myself now, sitting in silence and firelight. I feel my breathing even out, my heart slow, my limbs go heavy. For two or three long hours, we sit with our legs crossed in the cave and allow ourselves to just exist. I don't fully understand what this means or what we've done, but when we return to the cabin, I feel peaceful and quiet. Mother Siskin returns to her cooking. I sit down on my cot and watch everyone as they live their lives.

'Lady Serin,' says the willowy young driver, approaching with a slight awe he's never shown before.

'Yes?'

'Sorrel hasn't eaten today,' he says and I find myself smiling. Why?

'That's alright,' I tell him. 'Fill his bowl and I'll speak to him.' What will I say?

The driver does as I tell him and I find myself kneeling beside Sorrel's cot with a bowl of steaming stew and a few thick slices of fresh bread. I hold it by his head so he can smell it. For a while, he pretends to be asleep, but his stomach growls loudly and he admits defeat, opening his eyes and glaring up at me.

'What?' he asks and there's a hint of the hostile guard I first met back at Little Werthing months ago.

'Brother,' I say gently. 'Sit up and eat.' I smile at him and he frowns, then he obeys. I sit beside him with my own dinner and we eat together in silence.

'Lady,' he says, and I wrinkle my nose.

'I'm your sister now, Sorrel,' I tell him. 'Even the cubs call the Great Bear *Mother*.'

'Sister,' he says and seems to settle into himself a little more. 'Why did she...?'

'I don't know.'

'How can we get past this? How can I trust my own judgement now?'

'With time,' I reply, 'which I think we have in excess now.' He talks to me now, tells me how he feels, what he thinks, what he wanted and planned and what he now sees in the future. I listen and I say nothing. When he's done, he sleeps. I work with my companions to clean everything away and to prepare the cabin for night.

Mother Siskin wakes me up in the hush of pre-dawn and we pull cloaks over our shoulders and go out to our cave again. Our little fire is still crackling, the wood not yet burned away. I don't ask how because I feel like I might already know, though I couldn't put it into words. We sit in silence again and we don't get up until the sun has risen lazily over the lip of the closest peak. Then we climb up to where we can see the kingdom stretching off far below. On the horizon, Yellowrise is a little glistening dot and south-east is the sea, a mere sliver of light somewhere beyond my invisible village. Far off to the east are the little hills with their little rivers that once marked the extremes of my little internal map of the world. It's too cold up here to stay long so we find ourselves quickly back by the now roaring fire in our cabin. It's deliciously warm and smells of distant childhood with stories and laughter and father bending his bow over his knee to teaching me how to string it. I don't remember his face but I do remember his smile. I miss him, but I don't mind. I've always missed him; it's just a part of who I am.

We eat breakfast together. Everyone, even Sorrel, talks quite happily with one another and I watch and smile and listen. I sit and feel the weight of the spoon in my palm and the hard seat of my chair beneath me. Mother Siskin winks at me. What is it she's taught me? Surely, it's more than just listening.

It's still dark outside our firelit cave, sometime in mid-January, when I ask Mother Siskin about the Great Bear.

'What do you want to know?' she asks, tracing the grainy lines of her palm with a pale fingertip.

'Is She real?' I wonder, the first time in my life I've dared to put voice to such a thought. Mother Siskin laughs at my question though, as she laughs at everything, and my lingering nerves unspool in the pit of my stomach.

'What a question,' she crows. 'Is the Great Bear real? What do you think?'

'I don't know.'

'You're meant to have met Her.'

'It could have been... just a bear?' Mother Siskin turns her whole body toward me and looks me in the eyes with a clarity I've never seen in a human face before.

'Just a bear,' she echoes, as though hearing it from another's lips will put my words into perspective.

'Yes?' She smiles again, bright and affectionate.

'If you believe it, stand by it,' she instructs me, then waits.

'Yes, just a bear,' I tell her, making my voice strong like I do when I'm speaking to a crowd. She nods at that.

'The Great She-Bear is our Mother,' she says, her voice suddenly low and smooth. Some old part of me wishes the priest in my village temple could have preached like this. 'Her children are fiercely independent and she won't force them to ride on her back when they'd rather run along behind. Sometimes, however, we need a little nudge to put us back on the right path.'

'So you're saying I really was chosen? Even though I had no faith or hope or anything?' I don't remember leaning forward, or catching my lip so hard between my teeth, but that's how I suddenly find myself. Mother Siskin reaches out with gentle hands to return me to a more relaxed posture, her thumb running over my mouth to keep me from accidently drawing blood.

'I'm saying nothing of the sort, child,' she winks. 'The Great Bear doesn't choose favourites; she's a mother.'

'So I wasn't chosen after all?' The strange sinking feeling I find in my chest shocks me, since I'd never believed I'd truly been chosen, but Mother Siskin is frowning at me, though still smiling, and she sighs lightly.

'Serin, you have a lot to learn.' I'm well aware of that.

'You were a priestess. Teach me.'

Even after five long months of leading Mulberry's uprising, I still don't know where I stand with the Great Bear. I was raised to follow Her, as everyone was. Even when my father died, I knew She was out there somewhere. Even when the king's parties became more and more lavish and the people became more and more famished, I still believed, in my heart. What I struggled with was whether or not She was good, or if she cared, or if the Ursulaic Laws could be trusted. Now I contend with a host of newer questions, such as, am I the

Bear's Anointed? Am I meant to be leading this uprising? Will we succeed, or even survive? Will it change anything? I hadn't realised how much I wanted answers until I was sitting in this cave, staring at this fire, feeling my humming mind begin to settle, my itching feet finally still. Only when I'm calm do I realise how little equilibrium I had before.

'You are making history,' Mother Siskin tells me. 'You stand on a precipice, preparing to dive into the unknown. It's only natural that you question where you're going.'

'Where am I going?' I ask, my voice trembling. Instead of answering, she leads me up to the ledge where our view is and she sits me on a rock to watch the world.

'Does the sun know where it's going?' she asks me. 'Do the clouds?' The clouds are low, brushing the tops of the nearby trees. A creeping yellow stain in the east hints at the passing of night. 'The clouds don't know where they're going, because it's the wind that guides them,' she tells me at last, 'but they always know where they are.'

'Do they?'

'I like to think so,' she laughs. 'Do you know where you are?'

'I'm in the Invius Mountains,' I reply, 'waiting for help from someone I can't trust.'

'You like it here?'

'Yes, but I don't like not knowing.'

'You know where you are, what you're doing and why you're here. You're doing what you need to do, so you must be where you need to be. If you look too far ahead, you'll lose sight of the path beneath your feet.'

'You're telling me not to ask questions?'

'I'm telling you not to ask useless questions.' I ponder this for a moment, tucking my hands between my knees to keep them warm. 'Do you want to ask something useful?' Mother Siskin asks me, and I take a breath, then pause.

'How can I help Sorrel?' She beams at me. We go back to the cave.

'How are you so sure of yourself?' Sorrel asks me, voice low and breathless as he pauses from his sword fighting practice. 'Just when everything becomes more uncertain than ever, you suddenly have all the answers.'

'All the answers? I?' I laugh, but he raises his eyebrows at me, his mouth turned down in a scowl. I tell him, 'I'm your leader. I need to set an example.' Sorrel picks at his tunic for a moment, silent and reserved, before he looks back up at me.

'If I ask, will you answer?'

'I can try.'

'What if she's dead?'

'The prince-'

'The prince can't be trusted,' he interrupts. 'He's just keeping us here. It's the same as the last one only we can't cause trouble for him, up in the mountains. He's never coming to get us and we're all so comfortable, we're going to die here!'

'Good place to die,' I decide and he openly glares at me, so I backtrack quickly. 'Sorrel, we've done everything we can. All we can do now is keep strong and keep faith.'

'You barely sound like Serin anymore,' he snaps suddenly. He turns back to his fight and I'm left stammering, the end of the conversation so abrupt, I'm staggered by it. What do I usually sound like, I wonder? Mother Siskin is a wise woman indeed if I've changed so much since our arrival to be unrecognisable.

'Sorrel?' I call. He ignores me, focused on his now vaguely concerned opponent. 'Sorrel,' I say again, my voice harder as I turn the name from a request to a command. He rounds on me then, all dark eyes and muscle and leather, reminding me of the day we met. 'Come with me,' I tell him, totally unfazed, and I walk away. After a long moment of shock, he follows.

I take him to see the view. I don't know why. Below us, a small spot crawling under the mountain can just be identified as a small troop on horseback. Only twenty or so riders, I think. Additional guards, perhaps. Is the king getting nervous down there? Has he discovered our absence? Sorrel points to them, gasping softly.

'Something's happening,' he whispers.

'I know.'

After this, he doesn't shout at me anymore. He doesn't question me. He ducks his head and starts working on keeping faith. I wonder what he saw in those distant soldiers? He bows to me when we pass now.

'Sister,' he says, 'the Bear bless you.'

'And you,' I reply, and I mean it.

It must be into February before we get any words from the Invius Plateau. It comes in the form of a cloaked figure, running through the still night, banging on the door. By the light of the fire, we watch the tiny stranger shiver and quake in a chair. We boil water for them and they drink. We find blankets and they slowly begin to warm up. At last, dainty gloved hands reach up and pull the hood back.

Mulberry has a black eye and a split lip. She also has blood spattered across her face and her blue silk dress. She looks like a noble but for the blood on her hands and in her hair, and for the haunted, hunted look in her eyes.

'What happened?' I ask, taking her cold hand. She shakes her head, lip trembling, and says nothing. We put her to bed and let her sleep.

She wakes us all at daybreak, crying out in a dream. When she has risen and we've made her eat something, she cries on my shoulder. Sorrel sits straight and stiff in the chair by his cot, sharpening his sword, and refuses to look at her. We've washed the blood off of her and dressed her in one of our tunics. She looks better – the blood wasn't hers – but she doesn't look *good* by any means.

'What happened?' I ask again and she looks up at me with her big child's eyes.

'He's dead,' she says, her voice wrecked. 'The king; he's dead.' And she cries again.

It's a few days before we finally get the whole story out of her.

'You killed him?' I ask and she nods.

'Shut up in that cell, what could we do? But the prince was the key.' She casts a guilty glance over to Sorrel before she continues. 'I knew he liked me; most men do, and I know how to tell and how to use that. Poor Dunlin; I did break his heart, I think.'

I remember life back at the village now almost like it was

another world. I certainly was a different person back then, only four or so months ago.

Mulberry's struggling, every word inspiring a grimace as she speaks.

'He dressed me up and presented me to the king as his concubine.' Sorrel growls now, low in his throat. He's stopped working on his blade. Mulberry lets out a dry sob at that, but quickly composes herself. 'Nothing happened for so long, I was growing impatient, but the prince told me that the king needed to get used to my presence. I was given a hair pin with pearls on it; I had to wear it at all times. Then, that night, the night I came here, the king sent for me. I went to him and he... he touched me. He didn't sleep with me,' she adds quickly, seeing Sorrel's shoulders tense. 'He didn't have time. I took out my hair pin and stabbed him in the throat. There was... blood... everywhere. I could barely see for blood and it ran hot on my fingers and I watched the life drain out of him. Oh, Serin, you were right! He was awful, but he was human; I'm a murderer!'

Here, Sorrel stands. Awkward and hesitant, he comes and sits down next to Mulberry. She immediately reaches for him and he pulls her into his lap with an air of helplessness. She presses her face into his neck and is silent for a few long minutes. Finally, she looks up again. 'I was smuggled out by the prince. We're to wait until everything's blown over.' Wait. We've been doing that for weeks. We've been waiting all our lives; we're good at it now. So, we sit back again and wait.

# Chapter Nine

## Returning

Mulberry enjoys the simplicity of life at the cabin. February draws to a close and the trees high above us bend in a constant and powerful wind. The sky, the lake, the peaks and the circling woods are all that exist up here. The bleating of distant mountain goats and the whistle of the far-off breezes are often the only sounds to be heard. There's a strange peace up here, like the complexities of life have fallen away. Perhaps that's why the air's thinner; there's less to worry about, less to do. The cabin is sturdy and rarely needs work done, food is readily available and the woods are good for hunting. Come spring, everywhere will be teeming with life and foraging will be easy.

I used to plan my future, wonder what I'd be doing a year, two years, a decade from now. Today, I see it all spread out before me. The lake is clear and I feel like I can see forever in its glassy surface. I'm more at ease every day, more peaceful. I catch myself smiling all the time, for no reason.

It's working its magic on the others, too; they all laugh much more now. Mulberry and Sorrel go on long walks in the mist and whisper to each other, or they sit in silence together by the fire and watch the world pass by; they both seem to be healing. Old Mother Siskin moved on to the Second Womb shortly after Mulberry arrived and she was buried beneath an ancient yew tree up in the climbs. They said she went before her time, that she was too strong to have died so easily. I know that they're wrong; she was ready and she was glad.

There are fourteen of us now. Mulberry celebrated her fifteenth birthday by proposing marriage to Sorrel, but he swears he won't marry a child.

'Lucky for you, I'm not a child,' she shoots back, and kisses him.

I bring the two of them up to my cave and, though Sorrel's already seen it, I show them my view. I'm half expecting them to have the same reaction I did, to change, to pause like I did, but they don't. They're uninterested in the cave; it's only a hole in the mountain. They laugh at the view and point to the different landmarks like it's a game. They don't understand how big this is, how little we are, so I lead them back down and return alone. Mulberry tells me quietly one day that the view scared her and I guess I understand.

The willowy driver seems to miss his donkey. He spends a lot of time with our gentle pack ponies, singing them the songs he sang on the journey. He tells me they aren't the same; he wants to go home.

Everyone misses Mother Siskin. They miss her cooking, too. I sit in the cave in silence and listen to her voice in the wind. What is post-life? What is the Second Womb? I wonder if she's really gone, because I don't miss her.

Every morning, I take a few people and go walking round the lake. Every evening, I go to the cave alone. Sorrel comes with me once or twice; we sit in silence for an hour but he becomes restless. He tells me things then; his fears, his hopes, his dreams. He pokes my fire with a stick and laments that

Mulberry's so young, that he can't trust her completely, that she's gone so quiet, that he loves her too much. He's afraid of hurting her, of being hurt by her, of what their future holds. Will we ever leave this place, he wonders. I listen and he says I understand. I don't contradict him, so maybe he's right.

At dinnertime, round the table, in firelight and furs, everyone laughs and talks and sings. This, I feel, is life. This is how we live.

It's a shock when life is disturbed, when the soldier who led us out arrives to bring us back.

'The prince returns to Yellowrise to be crowned; the king sadly took his own life in his chambers. You can't travel with us, but you can stay in the castle with a few soldiers until you can follow.' Everyone seems far too eager to leave our little cabin, and the soldier was telling, rather than asking, so we do.

We leave for Yellowrise only after the new king has been crowned.

'He'll be good,' Mulberry tells me.

'I know,' I reply. She doesn't seem as surprised by my response as she might have been a month ago.

'Are you glad to be going back?' she asks me when we're riding with our escort. We travel twice as fast when we don't have donkeys and carts to drive. We're all on horseback, despite widespread reluctance. Mulberry's riding with Sorrel and I'm riding with one of the prince's soldiers.

'Glad?' I ask thoughtfully. 'Yes, I'm glad. One must always be glad.'

'Will you go home?' She's watching me with vague confusion. I shrug and smile at her.

'Our sister rarely has answers,' Sorrel observes, kissing Mulberry's hair, still with a sense of urgency and desperation, still fearful of further loss. 'But she asks the right questions, so we must forgive her.' Mulberry laughs at that, though it's not as carefree a laugh as it was when we were travelling in the other direction. She leans back against his collar like she always used to and watches the horizon. She's quieter than she was; sadder, I think. Certainly wiser.

'Let's stay in Yellowrise,' she says to Sorrel. 'You can join the royal guard and keep an eye on our new king. I'll wear a veil and call myself Mother Mulberry. I want to name our firstborn Nadir.'

'Whatever you want, my love,' he tells her and they both smile. The pain etching their faces seems to fade a little. Maybe they just look better now the clouds have parted, drenched in watery sunlight and glowing from exercise.

April promises a warm spring as we pause at Crossroads for a drink. The innkeeper winks at me, or else I'd have thought he didn't know me. When we enter the city, a great celebration is underway. I barely notice the famously beautiful buildings or the rich banners and curious delicacies. I'm tired and suddenly homesick.

One day, in a street, Mulberry telling the crowds what Lady Serin did for them, I see an old woman staring at me. She comes over and clasps my hand and she smells of tallow, her voice like the whirring of a spinning wheel.

'See how worry has aged me,' she sighs, holding me close

and trembling. 'You never said goodbye.'

'I didn't know I was leaving,' I reply. 'But see, I still have everything I left with; no longer an irresponsible youth.'

'My little Serin, all grown up,' she wails and kisses me.

'If you think *I've* grown up, you should see young Mulberry,' I laugh and I see in Mother's eyes that she barely recognises me. 'She's going to be married!'

'I never thought any man could pin her down for long,' Mother smiles, 'but apart from that, she's much the same, though gentler. But Serin, I never saw you smile since your father died.'

'I didn't think you'd noticed.'

'It was like winter in the heart, the way your misery sapped away at me. I'm your *mother* and had to watch you fade. I always held out hope for life, until I saw you wither, but I gave up truly when you left. When word got back that you were heading a revolution, I barely believed it, but hoped. How much is true, darling? Did you kill the king?'

'Perhaps,' I muse. I killed the owl, property of the king. Symbolic, maybe. 'Perhaps I killed him before I even left; I was never hungry once my anger was gone.'

'I don't understand you,' Mother sighs, 'but then, I'm not sure I ever did.'

'Are you in Yellowrise for the celebrations?' I ask now, changing the subject before she pries too deep. She shakes her head though and looks at me with life in her eyes I never knew before.

'No, I came after you, months ago. You had already gone off to the mountains, though. I missed you by days.'

We talk for a long time, sitting in the street and laughing, reminiscing, all manner of things.

'I missed you,' I realise.

'Come home,' she begs. I do.

Mother lives for three more years. She dies in her sleep and the priest tells the village that she's gone to the Second Womb. I'm still homesick, even now. I stand in our empty cottage and stare out the window at the mountains.

When I go to Yellowrise for the summer Solstice, I speak to Mulberry about it. Her husband is a royal guard and she, a royal advisor. She doesn't wear a veil, but their firstborn is called Nadir.

'You were unhappy there,' she says wisely. 'It was never your *home*. Where were you happy?'

I think about it, then I dream about it. I see a huge bear pacing outside an iron gate. I see a glassy lake and years spelled out like seconds or footsteps on a hunt. I take my bow and my cloak, my memories and a new pair of boots, I set my sights on the mountains, I take a breath, and I walk. Walking is like dancing, really. It's like hunting. It's like life.

*The Great Bear eateth when She hungereth after food. The Great Bear drinketh when She thirsteth after water. The Great Bear killeth when She lusteth after life. Be likewise as the Great Bear.*

# Appendix One

## Index of Ursulaic Laws (in order of appearance):

*The Great Bear giveth us a Leader and unto this Leader we giveth ourselves. Giveth thyself to the Bear's Anointed and by doing, thou givest thyself to the Bear.*

*The Great Bear eateth when She hungereth after food. The Great Bear drinketh when She thirsteth after water. The Great Bear killeth when She lusteth after life. Be likewise as the Great Bear and act only in thy need.*

*When winter weighs heavy on thy shoulders, all ye cubs, wait patiently for spring when the Great Bear shall delivereth up Her people; calleth to thy Mother and Her daughters shall provideth thee thy Sovereign.*

*When a cub hungereth, it calleth to its mother. When a cub feareth, it calleth to its mother. When a cub resteth, it resteth with its mother. Worry not, ye cubs, but calleth to thy Mother and the Great Bear shall cometh to thy aid.*

# Appendix Two

## Index of Songs (in order of appearance):

*While the Great Bear hibernates*

*Waiting for the cubs of spring*

*The She-Bear will not sleep forever*

*Joy, joy in times of plenty*

*Bless the king as he serves the Bear*

*The Great Bear rises for the hunt*
*and cubs no more shall cry.*
*Life is blooming, strength returns,*
*No thing shall ever die!*

# APPENDIX THREE

## INDEX OF LOCATIONS (IN ORDER OF APPEARANCE):

Serin's Village: *A small and vulnerable village on the south-western border.*

Little Werthing: *A walled military village with cobbled streets.*

Greater Werthing: *A walled military-orientated town with cobbled streets.*

Crossroads: *A tiny village with no temple at the foot of City Hill. An inn and large stables make up most of it.*

City Hill: *The large flat-topped hill on which Yellowrise is built.*

Yellowrise: *The capital city built on City Hill, it's made entirely of the distinctive local yellow stone and has famously beautiful architecture.*

Invius Mountains: *The large mountain range that serves as a natural border on the west of the kingdom, these mountains can be seen from miles away and are permanently peaked with snow.*

Invius Plateau: *The location of the king's winter castle, sheltered from the worst of the weather, this plateau is accessible from only one direction, is heavily guarded and has only one escape route, for emergencies only. After the king dies, the prince only stays there for a few months every few years with a small royal entourage, mainly to visit Serin.*

Mountain Lake: *High in the Invius Mountains, accessible only via the Invius Plateau, is an idyllic lake in a small basin. On the rim of the basin, a lush forest grows. Beside the lake, an old log cabin stands, built decades ago to shelter the king if ever he needs to make a hasty retreat from his castle a mile or so down the mountain.*

# Appendix Four

## Index of People (in no particular order):

Serin: *A young woman turned bitter by poverty and injustice, Serin has a fierce sense of good and bad but tends to prefer suffering in silence. A solitary and reflective person, she learns to see the complexities of morality and, having finally learnt to socialise, chooses the life of a hermit.*

Serin's Mother: *A widow characterised by her dedication to her craft, she spins wool every day, working to keep her beloved daughter clothed and fed. Forced to watch the joy drain out of her young child, she fell into a depression, only seemingly waking up when Serin disappeared on her adventure.*

Mulberry: *The vivacious and headstrong miller's daughter, Mulberry takes almost as many risks as hearts. She prefers recklessness to inactivity and often hurts people in her pursuit of satisfaction. The true power behind the rebellion, she mercilessly said and did whatever was necessary to achieve her goals. Moved by passion and cunning to varying degrees, she ultimately made huge sacrifices for the cause for which she would suffer all her life.*

Dunlin: *The shepherd lad who courted Mulberry is quite a nonentity. He loves his sheep and is very laid back and gentle. No match for his sweetheart's lively personality, the only noteworthy thing he ever did was accidentally injure himself at the temple when he was a child.*

The Captain: *A stout, sturdy man of middling age, the captain of the western tithe gatherers has worked at his job for several decades. Sometimes wise and sometimes suspicious, he has a kind heart and regrets deeply the task he has to do. He can only sleep at night because he is careful to never take more than the people can part with and his influence along the western border is part of the reason everyone reacts so positively to Serin.*

The Driver: *The willowy young man who drives Serin's cart is actually the captain's nephew. He has a close bond with his donkey and often sings to her, treating her better than he treats himself. Helpful and reliable, he rarely speaks rash words, but he loves a good joke now and then, often at the expense of romance, seeing as he travels too much to marry his sweetheart in Yellowrise.*

Sorrel: *A skilled and handsome fighter from Little Werthing, Sorrel was taught to fight from a very young age. Trained for the king's army by soldiers bitter for being stationed so far out on the border, he learnt to hate the man he was sworn to and became openly resentful of the crown. Staunchly loyal and naturally trusting, he has never suffered a loss or seen a real fight. He longs for action and offers himself readily to anyone he feels is worthy of him. This is perhaps why he loved Mulberry so quickly and forgave her even quicker. Insecure about their age gap of sixteen years, he waited until Mulberry was seventeen before he married her. Despite his reservations about the crowned prince, he ended up working in his personal guard.*

Old Mother Siskin: *A wise old woman with many a culinary secret, Mother Siskin was beloved by all of Serin's company. A witch by hobby since she'd retired as Greater Werthing's priestess, she was a vital member of the travelling party. She passed away happily in the lakeside cabin and was buried beneath an ancient yew. With her died many deep truths, of which her companions had absolutely no idea.*

Crossroads Innkeeper: *A wise man with a suspicious face and a kind heart, he learnt in his trade to be shrewd but generous. He reads people very well due to his customer-facing job and has a simple faith in hope and life. His eloquence and humble wisdom were learnt at the inn, too, though he bestows it rarely, preferring to listen rather than to speak.*

The King: *Although a pleasant and handsome prince, this man grew greedy and paranoid after his coronation. Decadence and pomp characterise his lifestyle and he has more personal guards than kitchen staff, all sworn in blood to die for him. Everyone hates him but his nobles, who respect him very little and would much rather attend his parties without having to actually speak to him. He trusts none of them and has come very close to starting wars by taking things too personally. His royal bird is the owl, symbolising wisdom.*

The Prince: *A handsome but cold man, the prince is as bitter and angry as Serin was before her adventure. Due to his father's many concubines, he has no idea who his birth mother is and the king's disregard for family and the Ursulaic Laws have created scorn and enmity between them. Having been raised by a nurse and a tutor, learning the Laws dutifully, the prince is vastly different from his father in all respects but for his piercing blue eyes. His loyalty is to the kingdom and he is willing to sacrifice individuals in pursuit of community gain. As king, his royal bird is the serin, symbolising humility.*

The Prince's Guard: *The prince and his personal guard are lifelong friends, having grown up side by side. The guard is the son of a nobleman and was granted his position at age sixteen, much to his men's disgust. Loyal and charismatic, he would give his life for his prince and his men, willing to commit crimes if commanded to for the greater good.*

Prison Guard: *Trapped at the Invius Plateau all year round, this guard has become embittered and misanthropic. Taking pleasure in the little bit of power he exerts over his rare charges, he becomes volatile if threatened or disappointed. After the Invius Plateau is left mostly abandoned, he goes to work at the Yellowrise Royal Prisons.*

The Great Bear: *An immortal she-bear of gigantic proportions and enormous strength, this god lives apart from Her people, only involving Herself when Her cubs are in real distress. When they needed guidance, She gifted them the Ursulaic Laws, a list of proverbs and customs designed to nurture wisdom and generosity. It is unclear whether She was actually involved with the Uprising of Lady Serin, but by general consensus, the serin finch was named the new royal bird to replace the owl. Theologians and philosophers often wonder, 'does the Bear hibernate when winter comes or does winter come when the Bear hibernates?' Her temples are scattered across the kingdom and Her image can be found on most bedposts, doors, storehouses and workshops.*